Super-tuned!

Story by Heather Hammonds
Illustrations by Mal Liddell

PM Chapter Books
part of the Rigby PM Collection

U.S. edition © 2001 Rigby
a division of Reed Elsevier Inc.
1000 Hart Road
Barrington, IL 60010-2627
www.rigby.com

Text © Nelson Thomson Learning 2000
Illustrations © Nelson Thomson Learning 2000
Originally published in Australia by Nelson Thomson Learning

06 05 04 03 02 01
10 9 8 7 6 5 4 3 2

Super-tuned!
ISBN 0 7635 7452 X

Printed in China by Midas Printing (Asia) Ltd.

Contents

Chapter 1

Nick's Hearing Aid

Nick pulled his baseball cap over his ears as he left the hearing center with his mom.

"I still don't see why I have to wear a hearing aid," he grumbled. "Only one of my ears doesn't hear properly."

"It will help you at school, Nick," his mom replied. "You'll be able to hear the teacher much better from now on."

But Nick hung his head and sulked.

When he got home, his friend Adrian was waiting for him.

"Did you get it?" Adrian asked. "Can I see?"

EAST COAST HEARING CENTER

Nick took the hearing aid out from behind his ear.

"It's so small," said Adrian. "It's really cool."

"No it's not," said Nick. "It's stupid. When I wear it to school, people will laugh at me!"

Adrian shook his head. "No they won't. It's no different from me wearing my glasses. If it helps you to hear better, it's great."

But Nick didn't believe Adrian.

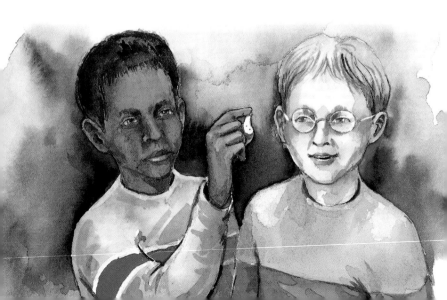

Chapter 2

What Music?

Nick and Adrian climbed up into Nick's treehouse. "What'll we do this afternoon?" wondered Adrian. "Go to the beach?"

But Nick wasn't listening. "Can you hear that music?" he asked.

"What music?" said Adrian.

Nick screwed up his face. "It's boring, old-fashioned music. La, la, la, de-da."

"Stop it!" laughed Adrian.

No matter how hard he tried, Adrian could not hear the music. He began to think there was something wrong with his own hearing. And then ... "Nick!" he shouted. "It must be your hearing aid. The music's coming through the hearing aid."

But Nick paid no attention. "Here is the weather," he said. "Today will be fine and sunny ..."

Adrian reached up and pulled Nick's hearing aid off.

"Hey, be careful!" Nick yelled. "I'll be in big trouble if it gets broken."

"Do you still hear the music?" asked Adrian.

Nick shook his head. "No," he said. "But it wasn't just music. It was weird; like listening to a whole lot of radio stations at once."

"It's definitely coming from your hearing aid," said Adrian. "There's something wrong with it."

He put it to his own ear and heard a high-pitched noise. "Ouch," he cried. "That hurts."

"You can't wear someone else's hearing aid," explained Nick. "They're tuned especially for each person."

"Well yours must be *super*-tuned," said Adrian, rubbing his ear.

Nick looked at his hearing aid. "Maybe this thing isn't so bad after all," he grinned. "I can hear all sorts of things with it."

"Yes, but they're all jumbled up," Adrian sighed. "You'd better tell your mom it needs fixing."

"No way," said Nick, grinning. "I can have fun with this!"

Chapter 3

At School

The next day, Nick wore his hearing aid to school for the first time. He turned the sound down, so he didn't hear the radio signals. He took his seat in class, hoping that nobody would notice it.

"May we see your new hearing aid?" asked Nick's teacher.

Poor Nick felt embarrassed. He took it off and handed it to her.

The teacher explained that Nick needed a hearing aid because his ear had been damaged from having lots of ear infections. One or two of the children looked sorry for him.

"They would be jealous if they knew what it could really do," Adrian whispered to Nick.

At lunchtime, Nick turned up his hearing aid. "Wow, a police car-chase!" he exclaimed, and he told Adrian what he was hearing: "We are in pursuit of the suspect, heading west along Ocean Highway. Suspect is driving a gray van. All units, please respond!"

But the sound of the chase was lost and Nick heard music again.

"What a shame," sighed Adrian. "Now we won't know what happened."

The bell rang, and they went back to class. Nick turned his hearing aid down so the music was softer, and got to work.

Chapter 4

Mayday! Mayday!

After school, the two boys ran back to Nick's house. The weather had turned windy and rainy.

"Whew," said Nick, fiddling with his hearing aid. "I'm getting a lot of interference. There's a storm warning out for all boats at sea."

Suddenly, there was a huge flash of lightning.

Nick grabbed Adrian's arm. "Oh no!" he cried. "I can hear something terrible. Listen to this." And Nick repeated what he was hearing: "Mayday! Mayday! This is the fishing boat *Bluebell*. We are caught in the storm and are taking on water. There are four men on board. Coastguard, are you receiving us?"

"We are!" yelled Adrian and Nick.

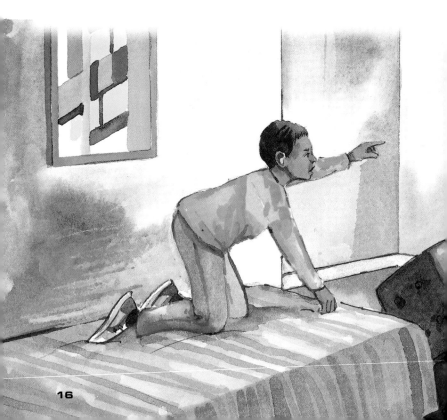

Nick's mom came running in when she heard their shouts. "What's the matter, boys?" she asked.

"Mom, there's a fishing boat caught in the storm," cried Nick. "They're in danger, and I think I'm the only one who can hear them, through my hearing aid."

"It's true," said Adrian.

Nick's mom looked at the boys and saw that they were serious. "You'd better tell me the whole story," she sighed.

Nick explained about the sounds coming through his hearing aid.

"Are you sure?" she asked. "It's hard to believe that you're picking up radio signals."

"Please Mom," begged Nick. "Just call the police and see if any fishing boats are missing. Those fishermen will drown if we don't hurry."

Outside, lightning flashed and the wind blew harder.

Chapter 5

Coastguard Headquarters

Nick's mom came back from the telephone. "A police car is on its way, boys," she said. "There *is* a fishing boat missing, with four men aboard, and the Coastguard hasn't heard from them. Nick, you might have to go out and help them find the fishermen. You may be their only chance!"

Nick looked at Adrian and gulped.

He suddenly felt scared. But he knew he would have to be brave to help those fishermen.

Soon two police officers arrived. They asked Nick to tell them what he was hearing at that moment.

"Mayday! Mayday!" repeated Nick. "This is the fishing boat *Bluebell*. Can anyone hear us? We are sinking. We have been blown off course and do not know where we are. We will set off flares. Coastguard, are you receiving us?"

Before they knew it, Nick, his mom, and Adrian were in a police car, speeding along through the rain, with the siren wailing.

They pulled up beside the Coast-guard headquarters and saw a giant helicopter sitting on a landing pad. A man in a white uniform came up to the police car and opened the door.

"Which one of you boys is Nick?" he asked.

"Me," said Nick.

"Hello Nick, I'm Captain Spencer," he said. "Follow me to the chopper."

Chapter 6

A Chopper Ride

Adrian went inside the building to wait with Nick's mom. Nick put on a life jacket and then took off in the helicopter with the pilot and Captain Spencer.

The storm had begun to ease, but Nick could see that the ocean was still rough; the huge waves were crashing against each other.

"Do you hear them, Nick?" asked Captain Spencer.

"Yes," replied Nick, pointing out to sea. "I hear them best when I turn my head in that direction."

"That's amazing," the pilot said, and steered the helicopter toward where Nick was pointing. "Our instruments aren't picking up anything at all."

"The voice is louder now," said Nick.

A bright light shot up into the air. "Look—a flare!" shouted the pilot. "We've found them!"

Below the helicopter, a small fishing boat was being tossed about on the waves.

Captain Spencer threw a big orange package out of the helicopter. It hit the water and exploded into a rubber lifeboat. The four fishermen swam over and climbed safely aboard.

"A patrol boat will pick them up," said Captain Spencer. "They're safe now, thanks to you, Nick."

"Thanks to my super-tuned hearing aid, you mean," smiled Nick.

Chapter 7

More Music!

The next day, after school, Nick was fitted with another hearing aid. His old one was being tested. Captain Spencer wanted to know why it had picked up the fishermen's signals, while his special radio equipment had not.

Adrian went with Nick to get it. "Hear anything unusual?" he asked hopefully.

"Just your loud voice," Nick laughed.

When the boys got back to Nick's house, they were surprised to find a package waiting on the doorstep.

"It's for you, Nick, from the fishermen," said his mom. "For saving their lives."

"Wow, a super stereo system!" exclaimed Nick.

"And with your hearing aid, you'll be able to really hear the music," said Adrian.

"I'm glad I've got it," said Nick. "You were right, Adrian. If a hearing aid helps me to hear better, then it's great!"